Juan's Story

by Kristi McGee
illustrated by Susan Spellman

Harcourt
SCHOOL PUBLISHERS

Requests for permission to make copies of any part of the work should be addressed to School Permissions and Copyrights, Harcourt, Inc., 6277 Sea Harbor Drive, Orlando, Florida 32887–6777. Fax: 407-345-2418.

HARCOURT and the Harcourt Logo are trademarks of Harcourt, Inc., registered in the United States of America and/or other jurisdictions.

Printed in US

ISBN 10: 0-15-351035-8
ISBN 13: 978-0-15-351035-9

Ordering Options
ISBN 10: 0-15-350602-4 (Grade 5 On-Level Collection)
ISBN 13: 978-0-15-350602-4 (Grade 5 On-Level Collection)
ISBN 10: 0-15-357960-9 (package of 5)
ISBN 13: 978-0-15-357960-8 (package of 5)

5 6 7 8 9 10   0928   12 11 10 09

Juan ran home and exploded through the door. "Mom! Mom!" he called. He was really excited.

"Sounds like you have good news," his mom said.

"You won't believe it! My story was chosen! I'm going to the writers' conference! I could win the state contest!" Juan blurted out in one breath.

"Congratulations, honey. You deserve it. I told you 'How to Hug a Dragon' is a great story!"

Juan ran up the stairs and dropped his books on the bed. He looked over the conference pamphlet. The conference would be held at the local college where his dad taught. Juan circled the lectures he thought would be intriguing. "Writing for Fun" and "Delightful Dragons" both sounded good.

The winner of the contest would be selected at the end of the conference. He or she would get private writing lessons with a special instructor and would receive a gift certificate to the local bookstore. Now Juan was nervous— he hoped his story would be good enough. Kids from the entire state would be there.

"Juan, it's time for dinner," his mom called.

He bolted down the stairs until he overheard his dad talking to his mom in the dining room. His dad said he was going to judge the contest. He would also work with the winner and be the special instructor! Juan couldn't believe it. It was pointless for him to enter the contest now. It wouldn't be fair if his dad were the judge, and if he won, people would say he cheated. Anyway, his dad might feel like he couldn't choose Juan.

Juan couldn't enter the dining room, so he stood completely still on the last step of the stairs with tears forming in his eyes from the disappointment. He listened for his mom to mention anything about his winning, but she didn't. "I wonder why," Juan mumbled.

Just then his mom came into the hall. She whispered, "Don't say anything about the contest to your dad, okay?" Juan nodded. His instinct told him she was right. "I'll explain later," she said. They went into the dining room and pretended nothing had happened.

Dinner talk was the usual. They each told about what they had done during the day. Juan did just what his mother said. He excluded the most important part. He said nothing about winning the contest.

Later that night, Juan's mother came into his room to say good night. He asked her why she didn't want him to tell Dad about the contest.

She explained, "Your dad won't know that you entered. That way he can judge fairly. You can still enter, and you can still win. Everything will be fair and square." Juan breathed a sigh of relief. He could barely wait. The conference was still three weeks away.

Dr. Ramirez, Juan's father, received copies of stories every day from all over the state. They crowded the mailbox and piled up on Dr. Ramirez's desk. Juan's story was in the pile with the rest. There were no names on the stories because each person had been assigned a number. Juan had to write that number on the top of his story, so his father just saw another number when he looked at Juan's story.

Every once in a while, Dr. Ramirez would read a passage from one of the stories aloud. During this time, Juan tried to avoid him. His stomach hurt when his dad talked about the contest. "What if he despises my story?" Juan thought.

As the weeks went by, Juan wanted to find his story in the pile sitting on his father's desk. He wanted to know whether his father had read his story yet. If he had, he had said nothing about it. Juan knew that snooping around was no good. However, he was still tempted. The night before the conference, his dad called his mom into the room. "Read this one. It is the best so far," he said.

Juan thought, "It has to be mine!" He wanted to read it, too. His mom made sure that he didn't get a opportunity.

"Time for bed, Juan. Tomorrow is a big day," she said. She gave him a look that was a serious warning. He knew he had no right to see the story. Still, he wanted to know.

That night he dreamed about winning the contest. "The winner is Juan Ramirez!" The audience clapped loudly. He came out of the audience and quickly made his way to the stage. His father looked baffled. Suddenly, the alarm rang and ended the dream. Juan jumped out of bed and got ready for the first day of the conference.

Juan had a great time. He learned so much about writing, including how to create an outline and develop a plot. He also read literature from some of the best authors of the twentieth century. Some of the activities were fun while others were hard. Juan made several new friends and proposed that they exchange e-mail addresses. Then they could read each other's work. Everyone thought it was a great idea. The second day of the conference was great, too.

That night, his dad was up late reading stories. He had narrowed them down to a handful. Juan walked past him on his way to bed.

"Can you give me some assistance with these?" asked Juan's dad.

Juan looked guilty. He stumbled, "I, um . . . don't . . ." Just then, his mom came in. His dad explained, "I just asked Juan for some help, but he doesn't seem too eager to give it. I could use his insights."

"Now you know that is your job, not Juan's," Juan's mom replied. Juan quickly ran out of the room, wondering whether his story had made the cut.

Finally, the third and last day arrived. The winner of the contest would be announced! After classes, all the students assembled in the auditorium. Juan sat in the back. His tapping feet were an indication of his nervousness. Someone asked, "Juan, do you have ants in your pants?"

"Very funny," replied Juan. He quit tapping his feet. Just then he spotted his dad, who was on the stage. He had the winning story in his hand.

After the introductions and thanks, Dr. Ramirez came to the microphone. "This is one of the hardest decisions I have ever made. You're all talented writers. I read funny stories, sad stories, and real-life stories. Keep in mind that you are all winners just being here. Hopefully, you have learned a lot in the past three days."

The crowd mumbled *yes*. Students nodded their heads.

"I won't keep you in suspense any longer. I chose the winning story because at its essence is people's kindness. I think it delivers an important message. Everyone should read it. Do you all have your assigned numbers? The winner is number 323!"

Juan looked at his number. He sat there dumbstruck. He couldn't move. He couldn't believe it. His stomach dropped. His mouth was dry, and he couldn't swallow. The crowd started looking around. No one was claiming the story.

Dr. Ramirez said, "Okay, maybe you don't all have your numbers. 'How to Hug a Dragon' is the title."

A friend elbowed Juan in the ribs. "Get up, Juan! That is you!"

Juan slowly came to his feet. He approached the stage. Just as in Juan's dream, his father looked confused. All of a sudden, Dr. Ramirez realized what had happened. A smile spread across his face.

"Well, isn't this a surprise?" he commented. Juan took his blue ribbon and the gift certificate. His father shook his hand. "Good job, son!"

"Thanks, Dad!" Juan said as the audience applauded. Juan realized that more than anything, he couldn't wait for his father to help him with his writing. He already knew what his next story would be about—a boy who enters a contest and finds out that his dad is the judge! Juan was not the only winner, though. His dad felt like a winner, too.

Think Critically

1. What is Juan's reaction to having his story chosen at the beginning of the story?

2. Why did Juan's mom suggest that they not tell his dad that Juan had entered the contest?

3. What is a word that means almost the same thing as the word *baffled* does on page 10?

4. What does winning the contest mean to Juan?

5. Would you have acted the same way as Juan at the end of the story? Why or why not?

 Language Arts

Your Own Story In the story, Juan wins a contest with his story "How to Hug a Dragon." The only thing said about the story is that it is about people's kindness. Write your own short story with the title "How to Hug a Dragon."

School-Home Connection Tell a family member about this story. Then read your short story "How to Hug a Dragon" aloud for the family member.

Word Count: 1,335